7284 5351

Ritu & Chandni

are getting married
& you are invited

Published by Yali Books, New York

Text and illustrations
© Ameya Narvankar, 2020

Connect with us online—
yalibooks.com

Instagram / Twitter / Facebook
@yalibooks
Pinterest
@yali_books

Library of Congress Control Number:
2020940847

ISBN: 978-1-949528-94-7

978-1-949528-93-0 (Paperback)
978-1-949528-92-3 (eBook)

Ritu weds Chandni

AMEYA
NARVANKAR

YALI BOOKS
NEW YORK

It was the day Ayesha had eagerly been waiting for!

Her favorite cousin was getting married and she was excited. Ayesha twirled in front of the mirror and admired her *lehenga*.

While waiting for her parents to get dressed, Ayesha made up a little rhyme.

"My Ritu *didi* is getting married today,
And I'm going to dance in her *baraat* all the way!"

she sang with a big smile on her face.

5

On the way to Ritu's house, Ayesha remembered the fun she had had at Deepak *bhaiya's* wedding a year ago. She had gobbled up mounds of sticky-sweet *laddoos,* and had danced with Ritu didi and her other cousins in a big, noisy baraat.

And now Ritu was going to be the first bride in the Kapoor family to lead her own baraat—a wedding procession with music and dancing—and Ayesha couldn't wait to be part of it!

Ayesha's mind filled with happy
memories when she heard her mother say,
"The tradition has always been for the
groom to bring the baraat to his wedding.
I'm not sure if everyone will be pleased to
see Ritu leading the procession today."

Ayesha could see that her parents looked
worried.

Ritu's house was decorated with garlands of fresh marigold flowers. All the guests had gathered in the courtyard. Walking up to the gate, Ayesha could smell something delicious in the air. But something was amiss.

She didn't spot any familiar faces in the crowd.

"Where is everyone?" Ayesha wondered. She couldn't find her cousins Tanya and Rohan, or her Deepak bhaiya and Tara *bhabhi*. Even her grandparents weren't there yet.

Ayesha finally spotted her *chachi*.
"*Namaste,* Charu chachi. Where is the rest of the family?"
Charu hesitated. "They are not coming, little one."
"Why not, Chachi?" asked Ayesha, confused.
"Well, they are not happy to see Ritu marry her girlfriend," she answered, almost in a whisper.

"But what is wrong with that? Why shouldn't she marry Chandni didi?" Ayesha blurted.

"There is nothing wrong with them getting married, little one. Nothing at all," said Charu, looking helpless. "It's just that some people do not understand their love."

12

Turning to Ayesha's father, Charu said, "Bhaiya, some of the neighbors have vowed to stop the celebration. We are worried."

"Everything will be fine," Ayesha's father assured her. "Let's lead the baraat as planned."

Just then, Ritu joined her friends and family in the courtyard. She looked radiant in a bright red and gold sari. Ayesha watched as her chachi painted a vermilion *tilak* on Ritu's forehead. Then, she helped Ritu climb onto a decorated mare.

Ayesha gushed, "Didi, you are the most beautiful bride I have ever seen!"

Ritu's face lit up upon seeing her cousin. "It means the world to me that you are here today."

"I wouldn't have missed it for anything!" Ayesha exclaimed, smiling back.

The band started to play a lively tune, and soon everyone was dancing! The baraat set off.

Ayesha swept up her lehenga and pumped her arms in the air. The wedding fun had begun!

17

The procession slowly wound its
way through the neighborhood.
People peeked out of their homes.
They had never seen a bride lead a
baraat before.

Some shut their windows with a disapproving bang. Others hurled harsh words at Ritu. Their shouts grew louder and louder until the band had to stop in the middle of a song.

Ayesha was shocked. Why would Ritu's neighbors say such hurtful words to her didi on this special day?

The *baraatis*, now nervous, walked in silence.

19

As they turned a corner, the baraatis saw stern-looking riders on horses blocking the path ahead.

"Ma, I'm scared. Why are they here? What do they want?" Ayesha asked, tugging at her mother's sari.

Ayesha glanced up at Ritu. She was
no longer smiling. Ayesha felt sad
that her didi was missing out on the
singing and dancing.

Just then, she spotted a second baraat
coming from the other direction.
Chandni didi!
She too looked scared.

The brides tried to move toward each other, but the riders stopped them from coming closer. The terrified baraatis watched as they uncoiled long hoses and took aim.

"Now!" shouted their leader. Ice-cold water rained down on the brides. The baraatis watched helplessly as Ritu's and Chandni's elaborate hairdos melted, and their saris sagged and dripped.

Ayesha too was drenched, and she began to cry. Through her tears, she saw Ritu trying to console Chandni. Ayesha couldn't bear to see her didi upset. She had to do something!

With all the courage she could muster, she walked up to the riders on horses and announced as loudly as she could—

"My Ritu didi is getting married today,
And I'm going to dance in her baraat ALL THE WAY!"

26

And she started to dance!

She twirled her lehenga and clinked her bangles. With her arms up in the air, she shook her shoulders. She swayed her hips and stamped her feet. Everyone was stunned!

Charu chachi jumped in and joined Ayesha.

The band started up again. One by one, the baraatis gathered up their wet clothes, and joyfully followed Ayesha's moves.

28

Now unafraid, Ritu and Chandni led their guests into the wedding tent. Once inside, everyone applauded and cheered.

The brides pulled Ayesha into a tight embrace. "It means so much to us that you are here today," Chandni said softly.
Ayesha smiled and said, "I wouldn't have missed it for the world, didi."

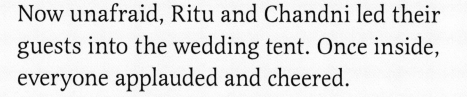

30

33

A list of Hindi words in this book—

Lehenga (lehen-gaa): A long skirt embroidered with beads, rhinestones, and thread; often paired with top called a *choli* (cho-lee), and a long scarf called a *dupatta* (dhoo-pa-ta)

Didi (dhee-dhee): Sister, particularly one who is older to you

Baraat / baraati (baa-raath / baa-raathi): A lively wedding procession with music and dancing / one who participates in a baraat

Bhaiya (bha-ee-yaa): Brother, particularly one who is older to you

Bhabhi (bha-bhee): Sister-in-law, your bhaiya's wife

Laddoos (la-doo): A spherical sweetmeat made of flour and sugar that is just delicious!

Chachi (cha-chee): Aunt

Namaste (na-mus-thay): A formal greeting

Tilak (thi-luck): A mark made on the forehead using a colored paste to signify a blessing, usually red in color

34